Sculpting with Physical Properties

by Barbara M. Linde

 HOUGHTON MIFFLIN HARCOURT

PHOTOGRAPHY CREDITS: COVER ©Pool BENAINOUS/TINACCI/Gamma-Rapho/Getty Images; (bg) ©Carl De Souza/AFP/Getty Images; 3 (b) ©Hisham F. Ibrahim/Photodisc/Getty Images; 4 (t) ©Photodisc/Getty Images; 6 (b) ©Leon Werdinger/Alamy Images; 7 (t) ©Astrid DI CROLLALANZA/Gamma-Rapho/Getty Images; 8 (br) ©Pool BENAINOUS/TINACCI/Gamma-Rapho/Getty Images; 10 (t) ©TONY MCNICOL/Alamy Images; 13 (b) ©Werner Forman/Corbis

If you have received these materials as examination copies free of charge, Houghton Mifflin Harcourt Publishing Company retains title to the materials and they may not be resold. Resale of examination copies is strictly prohibited.

Possession of this publication in print format does not entitle users to convert this publication, or any portion of it, into electronic format.

Copyright © by Houghton Mifflin Harcourt Publishing Company

All rights reserved. No part of this work may be reproduced or transmitted in any form or by any means, electronic or mechanical, including photocopying or recording, or by any information storage and retrieval system, without the prior written permission of the copyright owner unless such copying is expressly permitted by federal copyright law. Requests for permission to make copies of any part of the work should be addressed to Houghton Mifflin Harcourt Publishing Company, Attn: Contracts, Copyrights, and Licensing, 9400 Southpark Center Loop, Orlando, Florida 32819-8647.

Printed in USA

ISBN: 978-0-544-07325-8

3 4 5 6 7 8 9 10 1083 21 20 19 18 17 16 15 14

4500470116   A B C D E F G

Contents

Introduction 3
From Stone to Steel. 4
The Lost Wax Casting Method 5
Making an Original Model 6
Casting the Mold 7
Pouring the Wax. 8
Preparing the Wax Model and Making the Ceramic Shell . . . 9
Losing the Wax. 10
Adding the Molten Bronze 11
Finishing the Piece 12
Lost Wax Casting Today 13
Responding. 14
Glossary 15

Vocabulary

physical property
matter
liquid
solid
temperature

gas
change of state
volume
mass
density

Stretch Vocabulary

casting
mold
foundry
homogenous
 mixtures

molten

Introduction

A stone lion guarding a doorway. A metal soldier on horseback in a city park. A small silver charm on a bracelet. What do all of these things have in common? They are all sculptures. A sculpture is a three-dimensional object carved or shaped out of a material such as stone, wood, marble, clay, or metal.

Sculptures are made by artists and craftspeople called sculptors. Some sculptors make works of fine art that are exhibited in museums or other public places. Other sculptors design tools and decorations that you might buy.

All sculptors have to understand how to use the physical properties of matter. Matter is anything that has mass and takes up space. It has physical properties such as hardness, color, taste, size, shape, odor, texture, and temperature.

Let's find out how sculptors use some of the physical properties of matter to make sculptures.

Sculptors use many materials to make their works of art.

From Stone to Steel

Sculpture is one of the oldest forms of art. Sculptors have been working and producing since the Stone Age. These early artists used stone tools. Some carved small animals out of bones, stones, or ivory. Others carved huge statues and columns from stone.

The Italian artist Michelangelo lived from 1475–1564. He carved dramatic, realistic statues of people from huge blocks of marble. Many of his works are still on display in museums.

At 93 meters (305 feet) high, the Statue of Liberty is one of the largest sculpted images in the world! Auguste Bartholdi, a French sculptor, designed it. He attached sheets of copper to a steel skeleton in order to make this famous monument.

The Statue of Liberty is one of the world's most famous monuments.

The Lost Wax Casting Method

Some sculptors work with metals. Gold, silver, brass, bronze, copper, and tin are among the metals that sculptors most often use.

Sculptors who work with metals often use a method called lost wax casting. *Casting* means forming something by pouring a soft material into a container.

The lost wax casting method has been handed down from ancient times. The Egyptians, Chinese, Maya, Aztecs, and West Africans all used it. They made goblets, jewelry, and statues.

People forgot about the lost wax casting process for many years. But in the 1500s, an Italian sculptor named Benvenuto Cellini rediscovered it. He used the process to make his sculptures, and his work made the process famous once again.

Frederick Remington was a talented American sculptor during the mid to late 1800s. He used the lost wax casting process to make realistic statues of cowboys and Native Americans on the Western plains.

If you are ever in Washington, D. C., be sure to see the two bronze statues of Thomas Jefferson. One is in the Capitol. The other statue is in the Jefferson Memorial. Both of these larger-than-life statues were made using the lost wax casting technique.

Making an Original Model

The first step in producing a sculpture using lost wax casting is to make an original model. The model is a first version of the sculpture. It shows what the sculpture will look like, in every detail. A sculptor might take photographs or make drawings before starting on the model.

To show fine details and texture, the model needs to be made of a material that can be easily carved. The sculptor needs to think about physical properties of hardness and softness. The material can't be too hard to shape. It also can't be too soft, or it will not set, or harden enough. Most sculptors make models out of wax, clay, or another pliable, or bendable, material. If the sculpture is going to be a realistic figure of a boy, the model will need to show the folds in the clothing, the waviness of the hair, and even the details in the boy's shoes.

The original model includes all of the details that will be a part of the finished sculpture.

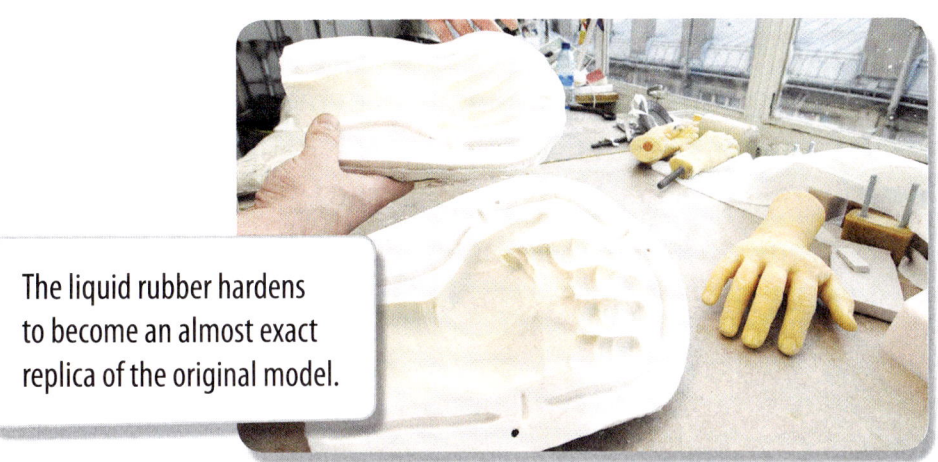

The liquid rubber hardens to become an almost exact replica of the original model.

Casting the Mold

When a sculptor has finished making the model for a sculpture, it is sent to a foundry, a factory that melts or shapes metal.

First, a mold is made from the model. The process of making the mold is called casting. The mold will consist of two layers, so that the mold will be in two pieces.

A foundry worker paints a thick liquid rubber onto the model, completely covering it. This rubber coating becomes the inner, flexible mold. After the rubber dries, an outer coating of plaster or fiberglass is applied. The mold hardens to a solid as it dries. Then, the mold is opened, and the original model is removed from inside. The hardened rubber mold is an almost exact replica, or copy, of the original model.

Pouring the Wax

The pieces of the plaster and rubber mold are assembled back into a three-dimensional form. Next, solid wax is heated to a temperature of 98.8 °C (210 °F). The wax changes states and becomes a liquid. This hot liquid wax is poured into the mold in layers. The mold is carefully and slowly turned, or rotated, as the wax is poured. Excess wax is poured out. After a layer of hot wax cools and becomes solid, another layer is added. Several layers are applied in this way until a wax shell has been formed. This wax shell is now about 0.47 cm (3/16 in) thick.

After the wax dries and cools, the outer plaster layer of the mold, which is rigid, is removed. Then the inner rubber mold, which is flexible, is peeled off. The wax replica is hollow. Like the rubber mold, it's an almost exact duplicate of the original model.

The wax pattern is a duplicate of the original model.

Preparing the Wax Model and Making the Ceramic Shell

The wax replica, or copy, is now taken to a section of the foundry called the chasing room. Foundry workers or the sculptor start the step called chasing. Their goal is to make the copy look exactly like the original model.

First, they closely examine the replica and compare it to the original. The seam lines from the wax mold are carefully rubbed off. Details from the original are added. Any bubbles that might be in the wax are removed.

The wax model is mounted, or put on a wax cup or handle. Wax tubes are added in several places. The tubes are needed for a later part of the process. They will create pathways that allow the hot, liquid bronze to be poured into the mold. They will also allow gases and air to escape.

The wax replica is taken to a part of the foundry called the slurry room. Slurry is a liquid mixture of sand and plaster. The wax replica is dipped into the vat of slurry and then into a vat of another type of sand. After each dipping, the replica is hung up to dry. Up to seven layers of slurry may be used. The process is repeated for as many as eight days, until there is enough slurry on the replica. The finished slurry is called the ceramic shell. This shell is about 1.27 cm (1/2 inch) thick.

The ceramic mold is heated to a very high temperature.

Losing the Wax

When the ceramic shell is fully dry, it's taken to the burnout kiln. A kiln is a type of furnace that can be heated to a very high temperature for a long period of time. The kiln is usually heated to a temperature of 850 ºC (1562 ºF). The high temperature and lengthy amount of time allow all of the wax to melt and drain out of the mold. This is where the name "lost wax casting" comes from. That wax is "lost" as it gradually melts and drains away.

When all the wax has melted out, the ceramic shell is hollow. It is then reheated in the furnace to remove any moisture.

Adding the Molten Bronze

Now it's time to pour metal inside the hollow ceramic shell. A type of metal that is often used with the lost wax process is bronze. Bronze is a homogenous mixture of copper and tin. When the two metals are combined, their properties are uniform, or the same, throughout the mixture. Copper is a soft metal, while tin is brittle, or breaks easily. Bronze is harder than copper or tin, and it is not brittle. The physical properties of bronze make it a good material to use for sculpture and other artwork.

Many foundries make their own bronze. Ingots, or chunks, of solid copper and tin are put into a container. The container is placed in a furnace and heated to about 926.6 ºC (1700 ºF.) The ingots melt, and the bronze is now in a molten or hot, liquid state.

The ceramic shell is also placed in a furnace. It's heated to 1150 ºC (2200 ºF). Now the molten bronze is poured into the hollow ceramic shell. The metal fills up all of the spaces in the shell.

The volume of the bronze that is poured into the shell is the same as the volume of the wax that used to be in the shell. The mass of the bronze is greater than the mass of the wax because the bronze has a greater density.

Finishing the Piece

As the shell cools, the bronze changes back to a solid. Once the bronze is completely cooled, workers break off the shell. Sometimes the shell cracks by itself, and the workers simply remove the pieces.

Is the sculpture finished yet? Not quite. Next it is taken to the metal room. The sculpture goes through another chasing process like the earlier one. The piece is carefully inspected and air bubbles or flaws are removed. If the sculpture was cast in pieces, as most large sculptures are, the pieces now need to be welded together.

Finally, the metal sculpture is polished. The sculptor makes sure the sculpture is as perfect as possible. It should now be an exact duplicate of the original mold.

The sculpture is finally ready for the last part of the process. This is called the patina, or aging process. The sculpture is heated with a torch. Then, acids are applied with a brush. The bronze changes color, depending on which kind of acid is used. The sculpture might turn red, black, brown, or blue-green. The final step is to brush on a liquid to protect the sculpture. When the liquid is dry, the process is complete. From start to finish, the entire lost wax casting process for a bronze sculpture can take from 8 to 16 weeks.

Lost Wax Casting Today

Ashanti artists in Krofofrom, Ghana, are especially skilled with using the lost wax casting process. Softened beeswax is used for the original model. Powdered charcoal, water, and clay are mixed to create the slurry. Replicas of ancient tribal masks are one of the specialties of these artists, who also make statues, jewelry, and buckles.

Jewelers often use lost wax casting when they make gold or silver rings, earrings, bracelets, belt buckles, charms, or goblets. The process includes the same steps that are used to make a sculpture. For smaller jewelry pieces, parts of the process may take less time.

The next time you see a metal statue or a piece of jewelry, look carefully. The artist probably used the lost wax casting process to make it!

The Ashanti sculptors make beautiful pieces by using the lost wax casting process.

13

Responding

Measure Physical Properties

Find two or three examples of sculpture in your home, school, or community. Remember that many things are sculptures: coins, ceramics, statues, metal jewelry, and other things you may see every day. Record two or three physical properties of each object, such as hardness, color, texture, and temperature. Make a chart to record your results.

Research the Science of Art

The visual arts, such as drawing, painting, and sculpture, all have a lot more to do with science than you might think! After all, art uses materials, and materials have physical properties. What are crayons made of? How do watercolor paints get their colors? What's the "lead" in a pencil? Where does clay come from? How is paper made? Choose an art material and do some research to find out what the art material is made of and how it is made. How do artists use its physical properties? Write up your findings and present them to the class.

Glossary

casting [KAST·ing] Forming something by pouring soft or molten material into a mold.

change of state [CHANYJ uhv STAYT] A physical change that occurs when matter changes from one state to another, such as from a liquid to a gas.

density [DEN·suh·tee] The amount of matter in an object compared to the space it takes up.

foundry [FOWN·dree] A factory for melting and shaping metals.

gas [GAS] The state of matter that does not have a definite shape or volume.

homogenous mixtures [huh·MAHJ·uh·nuhs MIKS·cher] A combination of two or more substances that is uniform throughout.

liquid [LIK·wid] The state of matter that has a definite volume but no definite shape.

mass [MASS] The amount of matter an object has.

matter [MAT·er] Anything that has mass and takes up space.

mold [MOHLD] A container in a specific shape that can have liquid poured into it so that it sets in that shape.

molten [MOHL·tun] Melted at a high temperature.

physical property [FIZ·ih·kuhl PRAHP·er·tee] A characteristic of matter that you can observe or measure directly.

solid [SAHL·id] The state of matter that has a definite shape and a definite volume.

temperature [TEM·pur·uh·chur] A measure of how hot or cold something is.

volume [VAHL·yoom] The amount of space that an object takes up.